Faith Parenting Guide

Stretch's Treasure Hunt

Thankfulness: My child is learning to be more thankful for the special things s/he has.

Sound: Read the story aloud and imagine all the sounds. You might imitate the storm that came up in Noah's Park. Then imitate the sound of the animals as they cleaned up the park and looked for the treasure. Then, consider the sound of the squabble that erupts among the animals. Think about sound as something to treasure. Ask your child what sounds make them feel good? Music playing, people laughing, birds singing? Consider the idea that there are many treasures all around us.

Sight: Fill a box with several things that your child might consider to be treasures. Give your child a minute to look at the things in the box. Then, take the box away and have your child describe the things in the box that are most treasured. Ask why they are treasures. Talk about the characters in the story and what treasures they thought they would find.

Touch: Play hide and seek. Hide something you think your child would treasure in the house or out on the lawn. Give clues as to where the treasure may be hidden. Have your child go from clue to clue until the treasure is found. Once the treasure is found, hold it in your hand and discuss what it is that makes the thing you're holding valuable. Talk then about the treasure of being loved both at home and by God. Discuss the Bible verse included here and talk more about the things we treasure in our hearts.

"For where your treasure is, there your heart will be also," Matthew 6:12 (NIV)

Stretch the giraffe looked up to see the dark swirling storm clouds over the hill behind Noah's Park. She called to the other animals to run for Cozy Cave, but the first raindrops were already falling. Before they could reach the safety of the cave, a fierce wind whipped through the Park.

Stretch and Honk, the camel, tried to protect the smaller animals, but Shadow the raccoon was swept up by the powerful wind. Stretch reached out with her long neck and grabbed the tumbling raccoon.

The wind caught Ponder the frog, too. He had been napping on his lily pad, and the wind sailed him and his pad across the water.

Screech the monkey swung down from a vine and snatched up the frog just as the lily pad slammed into a big tree.

Once in the cave, they huddled inside and watched the storm. Dreamer the rhinoceros, Honk, and Stretch stayed near the entrance.

The others hid under Ivory the elephant's big belly. They all wondered if anything would be left of Noah's Park the next day. The night seemed very long and very loud indeed.

The following morning the animals crept from the cave to find the sun shining brightly. The storm was over.

"This place is a mess," said Stretch, looking at the broken tree limbs and vines.

"Yes it is," said Ponder. He looked
sadly at the remains of his lily pad.
It was dangling from a tree limb,
almost torn in half.

"That lily pad was my home," Ponder told his friends, "and I don't like any of the others in the park. I need to travel upstream to find another."

"What will happen to us while you are gone?"
Honk asked the question all of the animals were thinking. Ponder was their leader.

"I'll only be gone a day or two," said Ponder. "You are surrounded by good and true friends, and God will watch over you."

As soon as Ponder disappeared up the stream, the animals heard a great crack from a tree near the cliff. A huge limb fell to the ground, just missing Dreamer. Screech and Shadow ran to look for bananas and apples. Stretch just stood and stared at the rock that the tree limb had hidden. It looked just like a monkey's nose!

"It's Nosy Rock," gasped Stretch.

Stretch had been
hearing stories about
Nosy Rock since
she was a baby.

Her father, Speckles, and her mother, Reach, had spent years
searching for a fabulous treasure that was supposed to be buried
near Nosy Rock. Unfortunately, they never found Nosy Rock
or the treasure.

Nosy Rock was right here in Noah's Park where Stretch lived.

Stretch organized the others into work parties. While they were working, she began to look for the treasure. At first she moved slowly, looking under rocks and digging near trees. But then she began to think about what the treasure could be.

Was it a chest of gold? Or jewels?
She became more excited.
She ran from tree to tree and even
plunged her head into the pond
to search underwater.
When she pulled her head
out of the water, her friends
stood around her.

"What are you doing, Stretch?" asked Howler the lion. "Did you lose something too? Can we help you find it?"

"Well...er...uh...no, not exactly. I haven't really lost anything, I just haven't found it yet." answered the giraffe. Stretch had an embarrassed smile on her face. She knew she was in trouble.

"What does that mean?" demanded Honk. "We're all working, and you are running around like you're looking for some great treasure."

"What do you know about the … uh … a treasure?" Stretch asked.

"I don't know anything about a treasure," answered Honk. Then he looked closely at Stretch. "Are you saying there is a treasure? Of course you are. That's what you're doing. You're looking for a treasure. It must have something to do with the silly rock you've been staring at, the one that looks like Screech's nose."

"Treasure?" snored Dreamer. He had fallen asleep, but he woke up at the mention of a treasure. "Let's find the treasure!"
The animals all started to talk about what the treasure could be.

"I think it is golden coins," said Howler.

"I think it must be a new kind of fruit!" said Screech.

"It must be something to make us look more handsome," said Honk.

Then they all raced off to find the treasure. Shadow and Screech looked in the trees. They ripped off branches and pieces of bark. Dreamer jumped into the water and dug into the bank. Surprised fish leaped out of the way.

The others began to dig all over the park. Dirt and rocks flew into the air. Flutter, the Dove, soared into the air to search from above. Ivory even began to uproot whole trees in her excitement over the treasure.

For most of the morning they searched wildly for the treasure. Then the animals began to get tired and angry. Each animal wondered, *Had someone already found the treasure? Were they going to share it?*

Shadow started throwing coconuts at Screech. One coconut missed and clunked Howler on the head. Then Howler threw a coconut back at Shadow and hit Ivory. Ivory sprayed them all with water from the pond. Soon all the animals were throwing coconuts and mud at each other. The treasure, for a moment, was forgotten.

Stretch, too, had jumped back into the hunt. She had looked in logs and dug a long trench through a bed of flowers. When the fighting started, though, she paused and looked around at the others. She realized that her friends were fighting each other.

"Wait! Wait!" she yelled. "This is all wrong! We're all friends! This is our home! Who cares about some old treasure?"

The coconuts stopped sailing. The mud stopped flying. All the animals stopped. They looked at Stretch, and they looked at each other.

"Remember what Ponder always says," Stretch reminded them. "God is watching over us. He loves us. We need to love each other, too. No treasure means more than that."

First one animal, then another began to laugh. Soon they were all laughing and hugging each other.

They stopped looking for the treasure. Even if they found it, they were afraid they would fight over it. For the rest of the day, the animals worked together to clean and repair their home. They picked up the broken limbs and coconuts. They filled in holes and cleaned the mud off the rocks. By evening Noah's Park looked even better than it did before.

As the sun settled into the hills, Ponder floated up on his new lily pad. He looked around at Noah's Park and smiled. "Everything looks wonderful," he told his friends. "I knew you would be fine."

The animals laughed.

That evening Ponder floated in the pond on his new lily pad.
He was very happy his friends had taken care of each other.
He thanked God for watching over them.
As he paddled to shore he bumped
into something in the pond.
He looked, but then paddled on.
Whatever it was would
wait for another day.

DREAMER HAS A NIGHTMARE

Dreamer the rhinoceros loves to dream, until one day he has his first nightmare. How will Dreamer handle this frightening experience? Discover the answer in the Noah's Park adventure, Dreamer Has a Nightmare.

CAMELS DON'T FLY

Honk the camel finds a statue of a camel with wings. Now, he is convinced that he can fly, too. Will Honk be the first camel to fly? Find out in the Noah's Park adventure Camels Don't Fly.